Stephen Ajay
THE WHALES ARE BURNING

Stephen Ajay

THE WHALES ARE BURNING

New Rivers Press 1985

Library of Congress Catalog Card Number: 85-060567
ISBN 0-89823-066-7
Book design: C. W. Truesdale
Typesetting: Peregrine Cold Type
Front Cover Photo: Courtesy of Barry Lopez

Our thanks to the editors of the following publications for permis-
sion to reprint poems which first appeared in them: *Confrontation*,
The Hollins Critic, *Ironwood*, *The Paris Review*, *Ploughshares*,
Poetry Now, and *Yellow Silk*.

The Whales Are Burning has been published with the aid of grants
from the Arts Development Fund of the United Arts Council, the
First Bank System Foundation, and the McKnight Foundation.

Stephen Ajay is also author of

Abracadabra
(New Rivers Press, 1977)

New Rivers Press Books are distributed by

Bookslinger	and	Small Press Distribution
213 East 4th St.		1784 Shattuck Ave.
St. Paul, MN 55101		Berkeley, CA 94709

The Whales Are Burning has been manufactured in the United States
of America for New Rivers Press (C. W. Truesdale, editor/publisher),
1602 Selby Ave., St. Paul, MN 55104 in a first edition of 750 copies.

For My Mother
and
For Anne

THE WHALES ARE BURNING

I

II

III

IV

V

I

THE EASIEST MAGIC

for Anne

I

We tear muscles in our
hearts trying to build the
tiny castle of a child's
brain

Each month like highway thieves
we wait camouflaged and merciless
at the side of the road, listen
for the route of the ritual
transfer

We talk only of this and your
temperature that slinks across the
calendar; like spiders we spin a
warning thread from our abdomens to
the trap. We wait. Again and
again it doesn't work

II

I take the crow's feather I found
yesterday on the shoulder of the
road and draw it across
my mouth

III

In the hospital you are put to sleep;
a stranger's hand creeps up into
your chamber, the beam from his lamp
blue as ice

We come back to bed and remember:
governments take women against their
will, end rapids of sperm with one
quick flick of a knife

We cut a template for a mile
of paper dolls, pat the bed so that
the dogs will know they are
welcome

IV

Yesterday when I found the crow's
feather, I found this hollow
sleeve of birch that sits on
the mantle; I stare at the vacant
skin that stands like the hood
of a klansman, turns to a fortress in
this empty evening

V

Tomorrow, once more, we will move
blind fingers over the wizard's
map; we will send the Tiger Salamander
who can live in fire but tonight we
must love each other like the last
tender creatures on earth

RARE GOODS

for Dennis Leon

Worn smooth this love for you could
   be sold in a shop; people gently
turn over this kind of china, dream
   a history of meals in the hairline
faults. When the buyer's fingerprints
   cruise the edge, he'll find it
intact—still it's old and few see
   the traveler, wrinkled, as noble:
this love packed up, jostled in travel
   lost or to be inherited--a utensil
of survival; so someone will spy it
   in a corner, ask the owner, he won't
know much but it won't matter.

CHAPULTEPEC

we walked just before
dark; it was hot
I don't remember english
or spanish; there was no
hurry, we held each other
at the waist, the pigeons
walked in front; we bit
petals of yellow mango
slick with lime juice
and chili and did not
dream of anywhere

LATE EPITHALAMION:COMPOSITE

for Anne

It's the white of the bed or the white of the page
that turns
the minute to privilege
marriage is just such
a tapestry of stains (the sky goes dark
and bright behind).

Outside the wild, ephemeral cotton-
wood seeds intersect in July,
the lungs of lilac collapse
as we police our fragility, as the ginger-colored
squirrel blurs beyond the screen this morning.

We kissed for three nights hidden in the
roar of the first-class bus: that first morning the solar
smell of burst Mexico rolled like dust from beneath
your dress as the driver pulled us off the highway,
hand over hand,
the windows soft
furred with the night air, night dust. Today I am afraid
of so many fragments: ("squawk the ragged-winged crow
lands on the bed and the sky goes white) before
my feet can touch the floor; a dream
rising like a fire, mixing you (my wife)
up with other men and women: your voice going
into that one's sleeping throat, the left-handed scholar
at dinner touching my arm as he lifts your
blouse over your head.

Tonight, again, I am a stunned
creature in clothes, the small madman who stares at
you, the small madman again stalled above the lovely
village idiot who grabs the flesh inside
my thigh, who whispers recipes. After ten years
the sun still shows red through our ears: a decade of
risings and settings and I kiss your small desert-colored
lips where the dolphin sings his Spanish, where the
miracle of shyness is awake in the room.

SHY

I come over to you in
   this poem
I bend over and kiss
   you in this poem
What do you need to know?
   What do you need to know to
let me do it?
   I'll answer for us, say
very little, "No!"
   And then I feel the weight
of your face.

AVALANCHE

I was on top, pressed into the scent
   you left at night on the shabby
bed. We were both on acid and you said
   the little Czech landlord had snuck down,
begged like a dwarf in the dark. I listened,
   counted the cinderblocks that rose, that
fell in the basement wall. I was stiff inside
   you, wandering in the snow, deaf with
the slow stomp of blood coming back through
   the drug.

SPACE

He bends his knees.
　　He locks his hands
below her hips.
　　He lifts as high
　　　　as he can. He lets
her down when he
　　let's himself
go. Does he set anything
　　fragile
in the grass? Free,
　　　　he waits for her.

WEIGHT

We
are in a
mill like two
gray
stones that
turn
away from
one another:

surfaces
tighten, sacks
of hard
brown grain
rise
up
in a silk
dust.

COMING TO IN HAWAII

At night in the yard
The bufos vault
Over fallen mangos, their
Bellies crash through
Leaves toward the bee
Hives where they sit like
Buddhas, eating as we
Show off, wet and long
Married in the warm
Air; the nightblooming
Cereus opening as we
Undress each other, two
Songs for hands.

ARRIVAL

I want you, you are
coming, the wheels
are turning; I sit
with only my back
in this chair; your
shoulders are coming;
you are driving
through a wind storm
of insects; I begin
to circle myself, I
circle in another
sky without birds;
I am leaning, you
are turning off
the road, you are
slowing, the window
is unrolling; we are
in the top of a tree
talking.

HOW IS IT

how
is
it
that
I

come
to you

impossibly
me
and you

shudder like
heat waves
in a woman's
frame

YOUR SINGING

When it storms
an ocean
cries
in the trees
and when
you sing
your wild, red
heart gets
loose in
your mouth: the tones
like the stems of
water lilies growing
up through
the dark sand, through
the cold springs.

A VIEW FROM THE STUDIO WINDOW

Smooth wooden
Clothespins
Hold a rainbow of
Underwear in
The wind

Your thighs
Swing back
And forth like
A chorus line of
Stars, invisible
In the bright
Sky.

AFTER TEN YEARS

when we make love in
the afternoon
your hair curls

(fog does the
same to it)

last night your
fingers and mouth
slipped around
each other like a flower

and I dreamt we
were relaxed
and old.

II

THE WHALES ARE BURNING

for Barry Lopez

They are smothering on the
Beach; they are whispering
Loud through their blowholes;
No one saw them come, fifty tons
A piece sliding onto earth off
The rocker of the sea they
Came, each towing the death of
A small city.

Cut out of the flesh of
Water they lie like men in
Iron lungs. They know nothing
In air; their noises are going,
Going; what they send out doesn't
Come back; in the ocean they
Know a salmon from a shark at
Fifty yards, here they are
Smothering with a blinded man's
Memory of color; what do these
Deaf heaps remember? Nothing
Comes back, they are lost without
Music, without noises.

The earth quakes with their
Heart attacks; they are smothering
On the beach; dumb and sad in air
They are smothering; the whales
Are deaf in air. Men throw wet
Blankets high up on their backs to
Keep them cool but they are crushed
By their own bodies: the delicate
Arteries and veins that run on their
Spines are shut tight with weight.

When it darkened that night, the
Stars were dull with the blubber of
Clouds; Lopez says their hearts
Were as big as chests of drawers;
Men went numb in front of their
Faces, the disc of each eye
Following them like a stroke, the
Breath of this dying sticking on
Their skins

Disease was on the fork of the
Sheriff of Florence, Oregon;
Syringes flashed and sucked in the
Night, teeth were busted free with axes,
Chainsaws bucked and sputtered
In flesh.

When the rangers came in green,
They splashed them with cool diesel
Fuel. While bulldozers grunted on
The dunes digging graves, truckloads
Of tires were dumped and rolled
Against their darkness, the salt air
Thick with stink of whales.

They were dizzy and dying and then
All smothered and dead, their hearts
Broken off at the stump. Tires were
Rolled right up to their faces;
Wood and tires mixed at their
Mouths. They had gone deaf. They
Smouldered and died out, stared
Us in the face.

At last under the torch, their
Neoprene skins caught and split, their
Bodies bursting into flames like
Dirigibles fallen in the Alps; men
Ran up close for a final look and
Asked, was it a mistake like anyone
Of us can make everyday driving into
A tree, the simple way to find another
World?

But the only sounds were
Their big souls whirling in smoke and
The best anyone could do was sit near
And bear the weight of their lives.

IN MOTION IN MEXICO

We could see a mile down the
    narrowness. I saw it coming—
we were speeding on the highway
    toward Guaymas when it started
off the hill, a wild-west inter-
    ruption, our clothes flapping
on hangers like flimsy angels as
    we passed the people: two women
and one child who watched still
    as the sky. It kept coming, the
angle of anticipation perfect from
    the start: something in the
wheels, maybe the spinning, was
    recognized. Finally when we
touched, his thin speed felt like
    a raised marker in the road, a
stopped weight.

THE CROW

Is mainly hydro-
carbons; fully
witted he flies
freely in
and out of the
trees. He lands
on the Spring
grass, bituminous
and out of reach.

THE MARCH OF THE SPINY LOBSTER

Over the mountains
of the ocean
thousands
single-
file
in
the
dark

At
dawn
they dream
of being aimless.

THE GIRAFFE

is
lucky
to live
two
years and after
that he is
all slick, thick
hoofs and little
sleep

A STRIKE AT JEWEL LAKE

So excited,
I tore the cartilage
half off his face
and under my wet boots
the log spun
backwards, the hook
staying as I towed him,
swaying like a kite
underwater, up onto the
shore. I bent over his
unflinching face, my left
hand pinning him to
the bank where the rod
had fallen, and I saw
from the corner of
my eye, the line
shining and limp in
spirals. I picked up
a branch and the first
blow came down
lifting up his body;
the second missed; I
raised the branch
again above his still
waving fin
these eyes trying to
recognize these hands.

IN THE SUNLIGHT

Curled in-
to each
other

the dragonflies
move side-
ways

they mate
in big
bows, sewing

up
the dazzling
blue

of their
next season.

NEAR LAKE MERRITT

A pelican
is approaching, low
alone, inside
Oakland; his eyes
sidle up and down
the sky—I am
in my car; I coast
close to the water,
his folded wings come
out high over my face,
his head tips
towards it; he skims,
calm, heavy—This is
a tide pool, brown
and cool; a shifting
sheet of dents, oil
and paper cups
float up close to
the rim of stones—
The gulls scatter as
he sets down, my left
blinker on: these
the connections in
air.

AÑO NUEVO, THE ELEPHANT SEALS

The rank odor of mammal afterbirth
Lifts off the sand. Logs of fur
And flesh notch the beach:
The young males, quarter finalists
Lie still with nothing to do un-
Til next year when the females flower
Again in the saltwater.

Up the beach one harem is
Left lolling about its Alpha-
Bull, his six thousand pounds melted
Down to four, his breath as
Clean as a child's while
In the surf, three of the biggest
Bob and trumpet some scenario of
Future domination; their white
Battle vests thicken as the final
Female is drawn out into
The squid-streaked bay.

AMPHIBIOUS:
"living a double life" — from the Greek

I found you in the road, a silent
hump of flesh
still and ecstatic in
the rain. Your webbed, rear
feet masterfully folded; the front
flexible as an infant's or
an angel's.

Separated—flesh from ground
I put you in my lunch pail, lay
down on ripped grass what we
were warned about: what grows
on the back
of an old friend. Finally I
saw you shift your weight, your
expressionless mouth, saw
your incredibly religious head
that rested in the crimped
metal corner-move—dark
and plump like heart. At last
when I touched the tip
of your foot
you started a long, hard
swallow that lasted until
I set you back down on
the drenched shoulder of
the road, beautiful as the
Buddha by the river.

SOUNDWORKS

the tree   frog
lives
near trees   not in their

arms   usually   at dusk or when
every blade and board
is cool   their   small, pink

brains
heat   up inside slightly

larger bones   stretched   over
with
green   and their eyes

make round dents in the air and
the sounds
of wet wooden bracelets

twisting:

back and forth
just before
dark

SARATOGA SPRINGS, N.Y.

Early this morning
the traffic sounded
like a band-saw working
slow through
bone. It might have
rained; a lone
cardinal pitched
himself high above
the oceanic snore
of unsold appliances,
cushioned California
peaches, the muscular
noises and whispers
of fresh horses
tied tight and gliding
in their trailers.

AT NOON

Katie, alive you're so
wonderfully old, the oldest
dog on the block. You still
adore the sun on your coat.

When you wake from a nap,
you stand up, sway and lightly
paw the lawn, half in a world
where your pups survive.

THE AFTERNOON OFF

It took
the cats meow-
ing lightly
for us to
understand how
mending our
house, fractured
in a fractured
city keeps
us from
bending over
each other's
naked body,
astonished by
the new
shapes of
asking.

III

DAUGHTER AND FATHER

for Sybil

I float in the cut-
off night, fish bones
stuck on the plates
it is late
they'll wait, I hear
you cough in your
sleep; you toss
in your child's bed
and creep back into
my head. Who cares
for the difficulty of
all the daylights when
you're as pretty
as an iris being
undone. But in
the wrap-around screen
of my skull, I see
you with your
first lover in the
nude, no one
asks a dance, speaks of
romance and your
father already hides like
a dinosaur; prepares
his mythic stance.

EXCHANGE

I have watched you walk
Slowly to school, still the world
Appears in braille; you reluctantly pack
Your clarinet in its gray case, you
See a white moth hug the porch light
When you leave.
   There is a tall, beautiful woman
Waiting for you on the corner
Near school; you cross at
The light: an empty jar
With a twig. Soon you will rush to
Meet her on the corner in front
Of the children who move
Such beauty under their clothes.

for Sybil on her
13th birthday

THE HIGH SEAS

It would be enough
to write this with
accuracy, without
aspiration.
I pretended it was
a storm and I would
save your life with
just my buoyant
voice; we talked
across the country
once or twice a day;
there were your
signals from all
the foreign places
where your mind put
in, where voices
hung on people's lips,
where they fought
below your porthole,
the soundings I could
barely follow. I pre-
tended you were not
beyond the limits
and this contact made
the difference, it
meant we were within
range, the nonsequiturs
that bobbed in your
monologue only friend-
ly porpoise. I said
I had plenty of line
and was ready to go,
I could be there in
eight hours, be there
at the breakfast
table with hot coffee

showing you maps, com-
paring crossings and I
thought you could pre-
tend the choice I offer-
ed was deep and attract-
ive and we would drift
to safety.

IDENTIFICATION

for Sybil

They say they'll need
the dental records to
prove he is the same
person but I tell
them the child that
was me has gone no-
where to live. He
hears his name call-
ing me out of the darkness; he is this
tangled clump of
weeds beneath the
snow. He comes every-
where with me in the
backseat of the car;
he sits on the floor
of the closet and lis-
tens to the thin
music the hangers
make, touched
and stripped.

DISTANCE FROM A NEARBY FRIEND

there is a thin,
very thin, board
in your face: no holes,
only a tangled
grain
that stares
and hums
when the wind
blows the gate
at my waist.

MILLING

words are
coarse
in the natural way
wheat
just harvested
is; even
threshed
and separated they
are rough/

rubbing them
between
bodies,
the dust
settles in our lungs
a sweet powder

THE EGG OF ANGER

I want to say I have
no patience, no talent,
no courage for anger "long-
distance". I want to write
and say you shouldn't have
either! You see I am try-
ing to get it out here; I
want to say, "you're not
that hard" (as nails) although
you know they keep our separate hard ends touching. I
want to say *I* rise like
silk grass in Thailand or
the Philippines and *I* know
the Oriental art of join-
ery; I want to say admitted-
ly it is a fragile craft with
history, where a person cups
a hand over his teeth while
laughing, or picking. I want
to say if we could agree
that there is no correct
starting place, then it might
be we have the same problem of
fires: one swirling out from
the center of the forest into
the sky while the other
creeps low, in smoke,
across the field
and finally after
hanging on this long, I want
to say slowly that it could be
in these distances where
the wind goes in both dir-
ections, we'll burn exact
and bright.

IV

WITHOUT COMPROMISE

After the bloody fingers came
loose one by one; when the dumb,
smashed thumb of Great Britain
came up; after Gandhi had slept
with his cheek against the bars
for years; when the skin that
kept him in a cage took on
the feel of parchment; before
the bullet flicked through
the matter in his life

he lay down each night with
two beautiful young women who
put his small hands right
between their legs and warmed
the cold bones in his bed.

TOLSTOY'S ESTATE

She held the small
head under; the
fingers moved
like starfish in
the weeds

Years later in
the morning, two
workmen began
to drain it, they
began to eat lunch on
a grassy bank, the
heavy one stood

up, shaded his eyes,
he ran down to the mud; he was yelling,
pointing at the
mud; he started in,
raised a short
bone, shook it but
they were every-
where like a starving
animal.

DIEN BIEN PHU, A COMMON GRAVE*

They marched him
to a small hill, the wood
of the handle as smooth
as marble. He started; his
shovel stopped in the
shoulder or nape
of the neck then one by
one the bodies came up
like tubers waiting for
Spring and then the order
came to take his time in
the blazing sun and when
he'd finished, another order
to slowly make each space
again; the features of
the faces gone.

*"On the long march to the P.O.W. camps, the Viet-Minh
singled out a French pilot, Capt. Charnod, to dig up and
rebury the bodies of civilians killed in a bombing raid."
—Bernard Fall, *Hell In A Very Small Place*

OPERATION RANCH HAND

Tonight, after more than a decade: cleft lips,
Cleft palates, absence of noses,
Absence of eyes, absence of forearms

Tonight, after more than a decade
The Admiral and his son are cool as idle
Gun barrels and the son recalls the wet
Deck of his patrol boat, maneuvering along
The river in the hot sun, the sun
Baking the backs of snakes, the back
Of the river, all the leaves

But this could be Sophocles, this
Scene on the news tonight, we
Know so much: the wind is blowing the
perfectly shaped leaves on the trees, blowing
The leaves against the picture window in
Fayetteville N.C., we can see that much; we can
See the Admiral's son, Elmo Zumwalt,
Thirty-seven years old, in a fine
Mist on the screen, in his office
Where he lays down the law for
A client, a lymphoma growing like a river
Leech in his groin, he knows that much

And we know the Admiral, his father, gave
The order to clear away the jungle before
His son reached the Ca Mau peninsula; his
Order leaving a landscape of stumps

May 7, 1984 THE WASHINGTON POST "... Monsanto, Dow
and the other chemical companies contend that the military
mixed together the Agent Orange of different manufactures, so
there is no possible way of saying which company's product
may have caused any veteran's particular problem ..."

On the news tonight we see
The Admiral's eight year old grandson,
Born with a birth defect; *his* father
Sits on a love-seat next to his
Wife; she speaks of what is
Terminal, she speaks of what is blank

May 13, 1984 THE NEW YORK TIMES   ".. major companies
involved in $180,000,000 out-of-court Agent Orange settlement
said yesterday that the accord would not hurt their 1984 earning
..."

Elmo Zumwalt stays out of the action, out
Of the suit, using he says, "... What energy he has left to
Build a strong financial future for his family ..."

May 9, 1984 THE NEW YORK TIMES   "... Investors are relieved
by the Agent Orange settlement ... at the close of yesterday's
trading Dow was up ¾ to 32⅝, the Monsanto Corp. up 1¾ to 95⅛,
the Diamond Shamrock Corp. up ¼ to 21¾, Uniroyal up ⅛ to
12⅝ ..."

Outside, a mist darkens
The view, a river leech
Swells, a sailor's knuckles tighten on
The rudder and here the Spring leaves tap
Against the glass where the clear
Blood of tears has disappeared.

SALVADOR AND THE COMING OF SPRING
AT BOLINAS POINT

Below us the unbearably bright
ocean shivers into the
land and the season wears
an urgency of seven shades
of green, riotous with poison
oak and purple lupine.

At this same minute owls move
without a sound in Chelatenango
as the sky darkens stuck in
the equinox; a child's crying
forming the rings of a target in
the moist mountain air.

Here it is mid-day when we find
two cars and a horsetrailer
at the trailhead. We have come
out a long dirt road to get
away from the news, a choking
powder in our clothes.

The trail twists inland from
the drama. Walking over flesh
colored rocks we hold each other's
uninjured hands, the wind forcing
words back into
our mouths.

V

THE METAPHYSICS OF STICKS

At birth our teeth are
buried: invisible seeds that
break the ground in rows.

In the light, each day
we become meticulously more
complex and hut-like.

After so many years we
circle helter-skelter, sticks
blown apart and separate

Bones catching their breath,
barely resting inside this
flesh—angry for attention.

EARLY MORNING

the stones
so simple in the snow
in rows

I walked back up
the road,
the snow kept falling;
it was early, the road
was scraped; the county
truck passed me
twice, a man
bundled threw sand
right, then left, from
the waist

the second
time, we
both waved; I was above
the cemetery only
a few of the markers
were covered. I walked

up the side of
the road where
the snow hadn't
melted, I
could see where
I had stopped to
figure the
dates—footprints

deeper and deeper as
they came close
to me

CONSTELLATIONS

for Harold Brodky

I am the younger brother, the one who kissed his mother's
    mouth. Now these are the extinct seductions
beneath the city, city beneath city, cities
    airtight, swabbed with honey—the dimmest black and white—the
telephone held to your head like my hand, one drop of blood
    standing on your lip, not falling—this lily-fresh consciousness
shakes itself out of sleep—
    in that space, in your pain, I became
the missing one

The sympathetic note sounding through our shabby
    house where I folded her, wide-eyed,
in the thick sherry of her breath, folded her nakedness
    into the cool bath where I saw the scar
that hooked above her pubic hair; it winked, dangerous;
    her whole body, alive and sober in its burden—
now she breathes her loving in shallow
    thimbles full of air. And I am compensatory, an organ gulping,
legs, young arms, live seduction:
    inspiring a response

to upper lip, tongue, this terrible fresh
    breath of consciousness shaking itself out
of sleep—scouting another flesh,
    trimmed frame, the constellations of fingertips
that repaint the dark. And where the end is open, where she pours
    her shallow thimble from daylights—the fulfilled wish
of her disappearance, an equation that places me in debt.
    How hard it is, this will and loneliness.

AFTER FLOWERING

It's about my mother and me (the plane has reached an
  altitude of 35,000 ft. above the perfect clouds)
but let me start another way:
                              the dull delicacy of
  the moth appalls us, the blossom of the apple
falls—while I'm aloft above a simple river
  of spelling reminded that an empty skin (you in
that classy hospital) is a shedding like the snake.
                              And while I sit in this
  humming body of gauges, I recall how gauze wrinkles
the faces of nurses, young as balloons moving
  from room to room.

I am the son married to your disappearance coming
back across the country. At dawn I see a syringe
  fill to the brim and the steel in this aircraft
whines as I think about our sequential ends.

                              Hard thoughts touch soft
surfaces (your profile in the live air): the thoughts that
  hit water like a bullet, white petals, beads—the deform-
ed metal that pauses, staggers and falls in a dream is
  my perishable and terrible faith
                              while the nurse
searches for the artery twice a day: (the darkest blood
  inside your arms like the rivers running below,
  meandering on the tops of your hands.)

Despite what I say of this descent, your thought is
the wavy contour lines of will, your imagination, a con-
  flagration that spans the bridge. ("That's Kansas City
                              down to the left of
the aircraft.") The thoughts: the smooth black wheels
  held in prayer as we get near—our lives twisted wrist
to wrist, a rope, the paired arms of acrobats, the hemp
                              of men and the smell
  of women: one with her receding view, the other
on this wing where the ground comes up to meet him.

SURVIVAL

A split in the meaning sews up the lip
   of the living. I come to the frail
but common nightmare of finding you.

   I locate a line, a new moon scored
near my mouth—in the mirror I am be-
   coming your wrinkled child again:
      a sack that floats
behind you in the fog. I am not comfortable
   here sailing on the slowest of barges
from where the dead lie still
      and the living cry.

THE TWINS

I saw
the wind tilt the corn:
Will and Humility,
just an image.

The sugarcane
cut at the same height, the
field freshly burned smelling
of flan, the bittersweet
roots in my house.

THE OBSERVER

a dream
wilts like
petals

sweet
and de-
tached